+A PICTURE BK-LETTER B
Pearl Barley and Charlie Parsley /
Blabey, Aaron.   DEC 08

+A PICTURE BK-LETTER B
Pearl Barley and Charlie Parsley /
Blabey, Aaron.   DEC 08

Pearl Barley and Charlie Parsley

Aaron Blabey

For my wife

Pearl Barley and Charlie Parsley

Aaron Blabey

FRONT STREET
Asheville, North Carolina

Pearl Barley and Charlie Parsley are friends.

Really great friends.

However, people often ask,
"Why are Pearl Barley and Charlie Parsley
friends? They are just so different!"

And they are different.

Different in almost every way.

You see, while Pearl Barley is very loud,

Charlie Parsley is very quiet.

THE BENEFITS OF WEARING FELT

While Pearl Barley likes to talk, talk, talk all day long, about anything and everything,

talk,

talk,

talk,

talk, talk, talk...

Charlie Parsley is very shy.

While Pearl Barley likes
to solve mysteries and get to
the bottom of things,

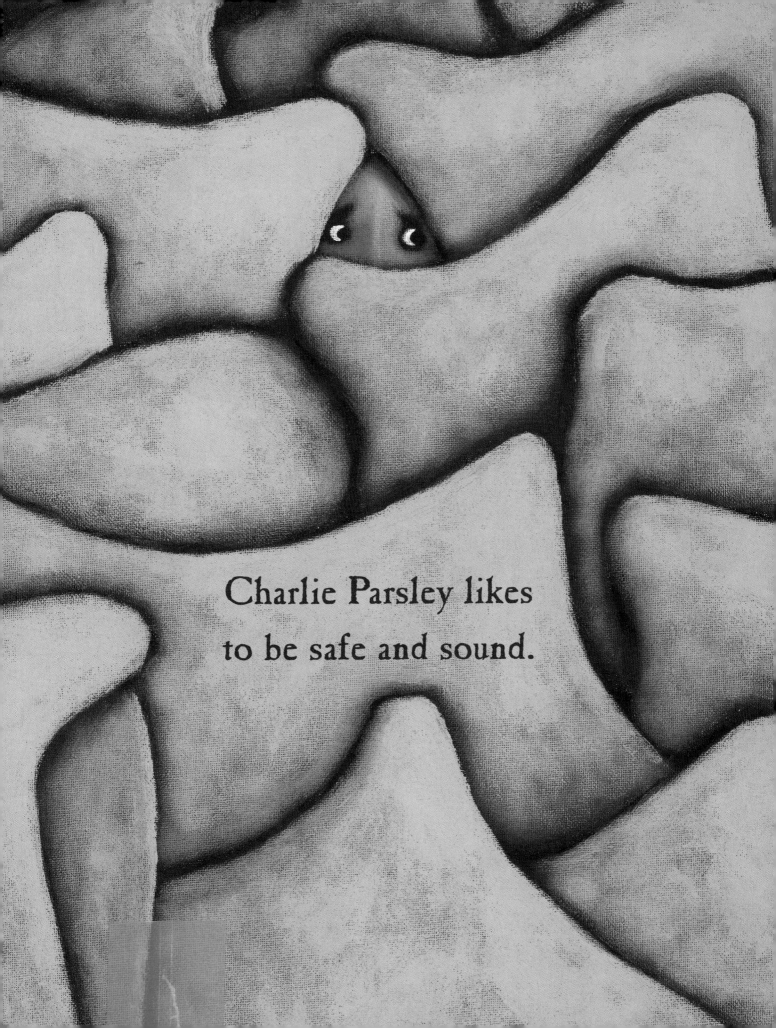

Charlie Parsley likes
to be safe and sound.

While Pearl Barley

likes to run amok,

Charlie Parsley likes to sit and think.

Yes,
they are different.

Different in almost every way.

However . . .

When Pearl Barley forgets her
mittens on cold winter days...

Charlie Parsley holds her hands
and makes them warm as toast.

When Charlie Parsley

feels scared of

scary things . . .

Pearl Barley makes him feel brave.

She's his hero.

When Pearl Barley gets tired from
running amok and solving mysteries
and getting to the bottom of things...

Charlie Parsley tucks her into bed
and brings her a mug of warm milk.
He has a lovely bedside manner.

When Charlie Parsley feels small

or lonely or just plain blue ...

Pearl Barley tells him not to worry and says things like, "I think you're great!"

If that doesn't work,
she dances up a storm.

Yes, they are different, all right...

different in almost every way.

And that is why Pearl Barley
and Charlie Parsley are friends.
Really great friends.

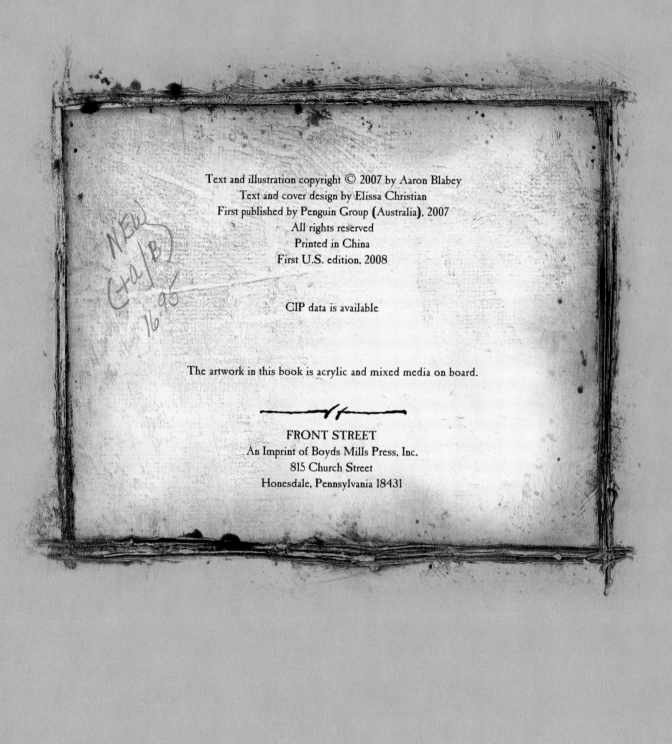

Text and illustration copyright © 2007 by Aaron Blabey
Text and cover design by Elissa Christian
First published by Penguin Group (Australia), 2007
All rights reserved
Printed in China
First U.S. edition, 2008

CIP data is available

The artwork in this book is acrylic and mixed media on board.

FRONT STREET
An Imprint of Boyds Mills Press, Inc.
815 Church Street
Honesdale, Pennsylvania 18431